A sensational murder trial brings a young African American attorney, Kevin Johnson to Briarton, Connecticut to represent a black drug dealer accused of murdering a Caucasian socialite, Charlotte Knowles. Kevin does his best to defend his client, even though he knows the real reason his two white law partners have given him this high-profile case is that he's black and so is the client. But is his client telling him the truth? And if he didn't kill Charlotte Knowles, who did?

His client swore he was innocent but as much as Kevin wanted to believe him, he wasn't sure he could...

"Matthew Cook, did you sell drugs in Briarton?" Goodman demanded, surging to his feet.

The defendant nodded, and softly answered, "Yes."

"You sold drugs for quite some time, I take it?" Goodman paused for a moment to let Matt nod in response. "Things began to get a little rough," the prosecutor continued, "Business started to dry up and you needed money for more drugs. You had a big drug habit, right?"

"Your Honor, I object," Kevin declared, rising as he spoke. "Whether or not my client has a drug addiction does not make him a murderer!"

"Overruled. The defendant will answer the question."

"No, sir, I don't have no drug habit," Matt replied solemnly.

"You needed money and so on the evening of February fourteen, two-thousand, you went to the home of Charlotte Hornsby Wainsborough Knowles."

No, Matt, don't squirm up there for God's sake, Kevin silently commanded his client. *It makes the jury think you're guilty.*

"Was the gun one you stole or one you purchased?" Goodman demanded. "Did you have a license for it? You found the victim in the kitchen, used the gun you carried there, and shot her to death. You then grabbed her valuables and money, and left the house."

The courtroom was so quiet Kevin could swear he heard Matt's heart pounding in fear. Or maybe it was his heart and not Matt's he was hearing.

KUDOS for *The Color of Murder*

The Color of Murder by Loretta Moore is a novella revolving around Kevin Johnson, a black attorney, who is what Moore calls "the token black man" at a prestigious East Coast law firm. Although Kevin's white partners give him some good cases, it does not slip Kevin's notice that all of his clients so far have been black...The story is intriguing and the plot has enough twists and turns to keep it interesting. For a debut novel, The Color of Murder is a very good effort. – *Taylor, reviewer*

The Color of Murder by Loretta Moore is a good debut novella. I was intrigued by the character development that I was by the plot revolving around the murder of the rich, old white woman. I immediately felt a lot of empathy for Kevin. Not only is he discriminated against by his white law partners (although you really don't see much of that), but Kevin also has to contend with his depression from his grief at the recent death of his wife as he struggles to raise his young son alone...Moore uses a lot of flashbacks in her book, which I found to be an interesting and appealing way to let us have more information about the various characters. I liked the idealistic young police detective, the cynical private detective, and even the scared, desperate drug dealer wrongly accused of murder. – *Regan, reviewer*

ACKNOWLEDGEMENTS

I would like to acknowledge everyone at Black Opal Books for helping *The Color of Murder* come to life.

THE
COLOR OF
MURDER

Loretta Moore

A BLACK OPAL BOOKS PUBLICATION

GENRE: DRAMA/SUSPENSE/ROMANTIC ELEMENTS

THE COLOR OF MURDER
Copyright © 2006 under the title of Not A Picnic by Loretta Moore
Cover Design by Jackson Cover Designs
Cover art copyright © 2012
All Rights Reserved
Print ISBN: 978-1-937329-79-2

First Publication: DECEMBER 2012

Published by Black Opal Books **http://www.blackopalbooks.com**

DEDICATION

This book is dedicated to anyone wrongfully accused of murder, or of any offense.

PROLOGUE

January 2000:

Oh shit! What the hell?" Gwendolyn Knowles muttered disgustedly when the traffic control cop waved for her to turn left and detour into the Briarton, Connecticut, downtown area. Coming upon one detour sign after another, she'd lost her way and ended up in a seedy, predominantly black section of town.

Gwen's eyes scanned the neighborhood, searching for a street to take her out of that scary place when she saw something that caught her attention—a familiar shadowy figure coming out of a house.

"Is that who I think it is? It can't be! Can it? Yes, it is. That's Tim!"

Timothy Knowles was talking to a young black man in front of a dilapidated building. The black man handed over a small envelope in exchange for the wad of cash Tim passed him. Then the two did a high five.

"What's with Cousin Tim and the black guy?" Gwen asked herself. "Hmmm, a drug buy. What else could it be?" She turned onto an adjoining road. "We just might have something here. This is valuable information, indeed. I wonder just how much Dear Timothy would pay to keep this quiet."

Two weeks later.

"Gwen, oh, Gwen, I love you, Gwen. Oh Gwen, Gwen!"

Gwen tried to stifle her yawn as her husband Brian Knowles screamed out his pleasure and bounced up and down on her.

She didn't think he'd notice her faking if she called out his name between gasps and sighs. Meanwhile another matter occupied her thoughts at this dark hour of the night.

She had to get rid of her mother-in-law. The woman was driving her crazy, always interfering in their lives. There was no doubt about it. Charlotte had to die. But how?

Maybe I could hire someone to play the part of a city utility worker or meter reader. He could arrive when she was taking her afternoon nap and hook up some sort of poisonous gas to her tank. Even if she heard something going on she'd think nothing of it. And if she was asleep, she wouldn't be aware of anything before she died.

But contacting a "hit man" wouldn't be easy. And adding to the difficulty would be the task of finding someone to pull together all of the things needed for such a complicated "hit." And what about Charlotte's housekeeper, Lizzie? The old bat was always there, snooping and spying.

Bad idea, dammit! Gwen concluded angrily. Perhaps, she could slip arsenic or cyanide in her mother-in-law's tea. *No, that might be traced back to me. Wait a minute! I know just the person to handle this. He obviously has the right connections among his druggie friends, and he can hardly refuse me. Yes!*

When Brian finally finished, Gwen rolled out from under him. "After that, my darling, I'm dying for a drink of water," she said, rushing downstairs to the kitchen. Then she pulled out her cell phone and dialed.

Tim answered his phone with a frown. Who would be calling him this time of night? "Hello."

"Tim, Gwen here. Listen druggie, I saw you the week before last. I know what you're up to."

A ball of ice fisted in Tim's stomach. "What do you mean? You didn't see me doing anything!"

"Who's that black guy I saw you high-fiving? You gave him cash, and he gave you drugs. Shame, shame, shame! Things like that will spoil the Knowles reputation. I think you're in deep doo-doo."

Tim listened nervously but said nothing.

Gwen snorted and continued. "We don't want the world to know that Timothy Knowles is a druggie, now do we?"

"What do you want Gwen? What will it take to ensure your silence?"

"Why, Tim, how can you *say* that? You know I would never do anything to hurt you," she purred. "But now that you mention it, I do have one itsy-bitsy little job I'd like you to take care of..."

February 2000:

The housekeeper, sixty-year-old Lizzie Miller, had screamed in horror on finding her boss on the kitchen floor when she came back from her day off. Her reddened face was awash with tears and she had been inconsolable when Briarton police, detectives, and the coroner arrived, soon after her frantic call. Head detective, fifty-nine-year-old Sergeant John Bowers started the investigation by questioning her son who had come rushing over to the mansion in response to a frantic call from Lizzie.

Brian Knowles, looking as though suffering from horrendous grief, eased down into the chair in living room. "Some valuables are missing," he told the detectives. "A few antiques, a couple of pieces of jewelry...small, portable items. But nothing major. Here," he said, handing over a scribbled list.

John looked at the paper and scratched his chin. "Don't seem like somebody broke in." He turned to the police officers accompanying him "'Nother thing. I noticed when the housekeeper let us in is that the victim's tabby shot across the door and raced upstairs. Go ask the woman where the cat was when she arrived on the scene this morning."

One of the officers ran out. A few minutes later he was back. "She says, the cat—Ferdinand—was snuggling beside the body as he always did, sleeping with the decedent."

John nodded. "All put together, I'd say the killer knew the housekeeper was off yesterday, and he knew the victim well enough that both she and her cat were comfortable with whoever came here last night. In fact, I think—"

A shout from the kitchen cut him off. As John started in that direction, an officer came running to meet him. "Look what I found," he said, holding up an afro comb. "It was lodged between a chair leg and the wall."

"An afro comb?" John turned back to Brian. "Did you mother socialize with any African-Americans?"

Brian looked stunned at the question. "You've got to be kidding!"

Ten days later.

The murder was over and done with, and it had gone just as Tim and Gwen had expected. The afro comb Tim had gotten from the drug dealer's bedroom, when he pretended he needed to use the bathroom, had been planted in his aunt's kitchen. The drug dealer Matthew Cook had been arrested and everything was going according to plan.

However, Tim couldn't figure out what to do with the valuables he'd taken to make it look like a robbery. He'd thought about burying them, but it was freezing cold and snow had piled up, almost a foot deep in some areas.

He couldn't leave the items at his house. Someone might see them and get suspicious. There had to be someplace he could dispose of them that wouldn't lead back to him. He'd just take a drive and find it, he decided as he grabbed the sack from its hiding place in the back of his closet.

His mind was whirling as he got into his car and quickly pulled off. As he was entering the main highway it occurred to him that the woods would be a good place to toss the sack of valuables. He turned off the main road and onto a country lane leading into the hills. Coming upon a small bridge, he stopped and parked at the end of it. He looked around but the road was deserted. There wasn't another soul in sight.

Tim grabbed the sack off the seat of the car and got out. He thought about walking to the center of the bridge, directly above the stream, but decided against it because he feared getting too far from his car. He didn't want to be standing out in the open if someone should come by before he finished his task.

Walking over to the wooden rail, he leaned out as far as he could, trying to drop the sack into the water below. But the end of the bridge was too far from the stream and the angle was off. The sack landed on the snowy bank just short of the river.

"Damn it!"

He saw headlights and ran back to his car, pulling away quickly before the on-coming driver had a chance to get a good look at him or his vehicle. *God, I hope whoever it is won't be able to identify me*!

CHAPTER 1

April 2000:

The late morning light streamed in through the open blinds as Kevin stared at the foot-high pile of file folders sitting on his desk. One of the folders stuck out from the rest. He reached over and patted the sides of the pile gently until the errant folder scooted back in line with its brothers.

"A messy desk is the sign of time being wasted," he whispered to himself. That seemed to be Robert Gordon's favorite new saying whenever he entered Kevin's office. Well, the fifty-seven-year-old senior partner of the Gordon, Wright, & Johnson Law Firm could say stupid crap like that and get away with it.

Kevin groaned and ran his hands over his close-shorn hair. He wished he could let it grow out, but a big, kinky, brown Afro wouldn't look professional. And even their token black man had to maintain what his bosses considered to be a business-like appearance.

He sighed miserably and turned toward the window, ignoring the cases on his desk.

Why can't I concentrate? I've got work to do, but I can't seem to keep my mind from wandering. I can barely put in an appearance during a case in court. And here at the office…

As he turned slightly in his Moroccan-leather chair and reached for the right-hand drawer of his desk, the small silver frame perched at the corner of his desk caught his eye. He picked it up and savored Chanel's amazing beauty—warm, golden skin, dazzling hazel eyes, lustrous, long brown hair, and the smile of an angel.

He stopped himself. Looking at her picture again was a bad idea. It just brought back memories of happier times— times that would not come again. Chanel was gone, leaving behind a six-year-old son and a husband who had adored her. He should have taken the picture home after she died, but he just couldn't bear to do that, after he'd kept it displayed proudly on his desk for so long. Taking it away was like saying she wasn't part of his life anymore. Maybe she wasn't physically, but in his heart he still ached for her. He still missed the sound of her voice, the faint, alluring scent of her perfume—*No, don't go there!*

"Kevin," Robert called from the doorway. Kevin spun around in his chair and gripped the edge of his desk as Robert entered his office with a folder in his hand. "I've got a sweet case for you. Very high-profile. A career-booster." Robert handed him the folder. "The accused, Matthew

Cook, is a drug dealer, who allegedly murdered sixty-nine-year-old, Charlotte Knowles, on February fourteenth. She was found on the kitchen floor with a gunshot wound to her chest. Cook claims he's innocent."

"The Valentine's Day murder?" Kevin asked in surprise, opening the folder. "Cook's black, I assume." *Of course, that's why they want me to handle it.* He looked up at Robert. *"Is* he innocent?"

Robert shrugged. "Your guess is as good as mine. Given his record, I'd say not."

Kevin wanted to ask, *then why take the case?* But he stayed quiet, knowing Robert would tell him only what he wanted to.

"There's a lot riding on this case—a lot more than meets the eye, Kev," Robert continued. "The victim was a wealthy socialite. I want you to do some investigating. Use the firm's resources however you feel is necessary, but handle this with kid gloves. There are some very important toes that could get stepped on, if you catch my drift."

Why? Could somebody on Briarton's spindly social ladder take a tumble from on high if the truth were to come out? "I'll do my best, Robert."

Robert smiled, almost condescendingly, as he purred, "I know you will."

Unsure if he was being mocked or praised, Kevin forced his mind back on his work, and his thoughts turned to one of his old cases—one that hadn't worked out too well. Against everything inside of him he had represented a sixteen-year-old black male who used a baseball to kill a young white man. He'd lost the case for the teenager, but he'd done his best—even though he knew when he took the case, he didn't have a prayer.

So why do I still feel so damn guilty?

Between the ever-present guilt and Chanel's death, Kevin felt an avalanche of emotion overtaking him. He was drowning. Some days it felt as though he was suffocating. He also had frequent panic attacks. But he had to hang on to his job in order to care for his son. Besides, other than Kevin, Jr., his job was all he had left. He just hoped he could do a better job for Matthew Cook.

Chanel's death had thrown Kevin into a dark depression, deeper than he could ever have imagined. It was as if a flood had overtaken him, drowning him inch by inch. He often felt as though he was deteriorating slowly, for all eternity, unable to give up and die.

Even now, two years after Chanel's death, Kevin still lay in bed some mornings, staring blankly at the ceiling and asking how God could have done this to their family.

But he had a young son to care for and self-pity wasn't an option. With a sigh, he went back to work. Each day it seemed he had to reach further down inside of himself to find the strength to go on.

He reached for the new case folder. Could he give Cook the best defense possible, or was it unfair to even take the case? He wasn't sure. But a lawyer was all he'd ever wanted to be, and now that Chanel was gone, if he couldn't even practice law, how would he ever survive?

May 1972:

Kevin was graduating from law school, and his family had gathered to celebrate. He bowed his head in gratitude as he looked at the pride on the faces of his relatives. Though not a one would admit it, none of them had really expected him to get here. They never thought this day would ever come. But Kevin had known since he was ten years old that someday he would be an attorney.

He'd spent his childhood in a big North Philadelphia house with his parents, Clarence and Julia Johnson, and four siblings, Clarence, Jr., Janice, Marian, and Luther. Julia's sister, Doris and her son, Maurice, and Ossie Johnson, Clarence's mother, also lived with the family. As crowded as it was, the home was always filled with love and support.

Their home was in an area where middle-class white families had once lived. All of the houses were three-story and large with elaborate facades. However, now the adornments were faded and many of the single family houses were broken up into apartments. Kevin could sense that it had been a better community when the previous residents had lived there.

When he was a boy the world was his to explore. Summertime was when he and his friends roamed all over the city on bikes. The wheels of justice fascinated him.

Something spiritual seemed to guide him and, as often as he could, he was on his bike headed for City courthouse downtown. He parked his bike at the impressive municipal building where cases were being tried and sat on the courthouse steps for long periods, happy to be near the action. He thought excitedly of how great it would be to work in a court room defending a client. He was sure that watching Perry Mason television shows had taught him just what to do during court proceedings. The day couldn't come soon enough when he would become a lawyer.

"Chile, I'm prouder then I eva been, you becomin' a attorney," Grandmother Ossie said jerking Kevin out of his memories. Her cheeks were wet with tears of joy. He was the first in the Johnson family to rise to such heights.

Until he became an attorney, Kevin had worked at many jobs. He would work in the evenings in his father's janitorial service business. He delivered telephone directories. And he was a summer camp counselor. At the neighborhood grocery store owned by an elderly Jewish couple, he stocked goods, delivered groceries to customers' homes, and cleaned up the store.

But once he started working as a law clerk, he never looked back. And then he'd met Chanel...

June 1998:

"Come on, Chanel!" Kevin hollered. "You can do better than that! Throw the ball to me, not to the beach!"

Chanel laughed as she tossed the beach ball to him. Four-year-old Kevin Jr. was shouting, jumping, and running about with his parents.

Kevin caught the ball, laughing and shaking his head. "Chanel, maybe you just can't catch! I know that you were the captain on your high school basketball team. But this is more like baseball. And, I was the top pitcher in grade school. Almost every time a no-hitter throughout little league!"

He scooped up Junior and pulled his wife to him. All three fell into a huddle of laughter.

The ocean resort called Sholes Beach was a broad, natural harbor, defined by dark-blue waters churning with ominous waves and a blue sky mixed with white, billowy clouds. Along the shadowy coastal surroundings you could almost feel yourself retracing the past. The shoreline recaptured the ghostly presence of Delaware's earliest settlers: the Swedes, English, and the other Europeans who began arriving in the early 1600s, as well as vestiges of pirates who came ashore long ago.

For certain, regions of the Delmarva Peninsula caused the imagination to run wild with fantasy and mystery. A hillock drowning with brown grass seemed to capture the illusion of The Man of La Mancha—Don Quixote dressed in armor atop his horse, Docinante, with the donkey,

Sancho Panza, at his side. The legendary figure was fighting windmills, while thinking he was performing heroic deeds.

The seventy mile drive to Shole Beach had been well worth the effort when Kevin, Chanel, and Kevin Jr. vacationed there. They'd had a great time. In their happiness, it never occurred to them that they would soon experience deep sorrow...

October 1999:

Tears tracked Chanel's face as she looked out the living room window. Through her eyes the world was a dismal place despite the luxurious colors of autumn in the foreground of her lovely home. She was losing her battle with Lupus. Just when she was in the midst of a dream come true—Kevin and Kevin Jr. and everything they had together—her life was coming to an end. The disease would soon take her away from those she loved. How would her family survive? It killed her to think of her beautiful little boy growing up without a mother.

Life brings you to the happiest level you could ever imagine and then drops you, she thought tearfully as she looked at the glorious scene outside.

The disease was stealing her life and there was nothing she could do to stop it.

Her thoughts rolled back in time to when she'd last been with Kevin to visit his family.

"Chile, we gone get you better," his Grandmother Ossie had told her. "Member when I had Pastor pray so you, 'n' Kevin could have a chile, and didn't Kevin Jr. come along?"

Chanel nodded 'yes,' even though she was beginning to lose hope.

"Chanel, I'm gone to go to the faith healer," Grandmother Ossie continued. "We gone get you well! One way or 'notha, we gone get you well."

Grandmother Ossie's faith was strong, but Chanel knew it was not to be.

April 2000:

No, it was not to be. Kevin sighed and pushed his memories away. Thinking of the happy times with Chanel and how much they had loved each other only made him more depressed. With a sigh, he picked up the phone. He needed to call the jail and make an appointment to see his new client.

CHAPTER 2

Kevin saw Matt's hands shake as he reached for the cigarette Kevin offered him.

"Mr. Johnson, I did not kill that lady. I never even heard of her. Don't know her family, nothing. I been out here in this drug world, mindin' my own business. I admit I like gittin' high, but I ain't ever bothered nobody."

Kevin had believed in Matt's guilt, just like everyone else, but after seeing the dismay and confusion etched on the twenty-nine-year-old black man's face, he began to have doubts.

Robert and John aren't bad men, and even though I am just their token black employee, they usually try to play fair. But I have to say they really handed me one this time. No case in the five years I've been with the firm even came close to this.

"I just can't believe I'm sittin' here in a jail cell talkin' about bein' charged with killin' somebody," Matt continued. "If it was a drug bust, I could see it. I been down that road a coupla times. But killin' some rich, old white lady? I feel like this is some kind of prank. I'm sittin' here wonderin' how did I end up a suspect for murderin' somebody." Shaking his head, almost in time with his trembling hands, he groaned, "This can't be for real, Mr. Johnson!"

Kevin felt a pang of sympathy. "It's alright to call me Kevin. I'm here because I believe you, okay?" He handed Matt another cigarette. "Now, you say you never even met the lady, and I believe that, too." He sighed. It looked pretty bad for his client, but Kevin didn't believe he'd committed the crime. "Do you know anyone, or have any business dealings with anyone, who just *might* know Mrs. Knowles? Anyone at all? Think hard, because it could be our best lead."

Waiting for Matt to speak, Kevin made notes on his legal pad. Someone had entered the socialite's home and murdered her. And from the forensic evidence, it was clear that Charlotte Knowles had willingly let the person in. *Just who was it, and why?*

When Matt continued to stare at his hands without speaking, Kevin stood. "We'll stop here for today. Remember, you need to be careful what you say and to whom. Don't talk to anyone without me present. Understand?"

Matt didn't answer, just turned his sad, tear-filled eyes on Kevin as if hoping he were a miracle worker. Kevin sighed and called the guard to take the man back to his cell.

Driving back to his office, Kevin decided to call in the firm's private investigator Peter Jacobson. He speed dialed the man's number on his cell phone while waiting for a red light. Pete agreed to meet him back at the office.

By the time Kevin arrived at his desk, Pete was already in the chair across from it, studying the case file.

"You've got a handful of suspects here," Pete mused. "Including, your client, of course."

Kevin hung his suit jacket on the back of his chair. "Who do you see as the others, and why?"

"The why's easy. Like my late partner used to say, 'Follow the money. Always follow the money.' Which means we need to look very carefully at the relatives."

Kevin nodded. "Well, the victim *was* a wealthy widow."

Pete snorted. "You're kidding," he teased. "With a name like Charlotte Hornsby Wainsborough Knowles, you could hardly expect her to be anything else."

"Right." Kevin pulled out his notes. "Let's see...she and her husband, Wallace, had one son, Brian—married to a Gwendolyn Harmon Knowles. The son would likely be the one to inherit. Though, of course, that gives the wife a motive as well. They have two children, Jessica and Alfred, ages sixteen and fourteen."

Pete arched an eyebrow. "A little young to be knocking off the grandmother for petty cash, don't you think?"

"Not necessarily," Kevin replied. "However, getting the gun probably would've presented quite a challenge for such high-society kids."

"Don't you believe it," Pete said with another snort. "A rich kid wants a gun, he just takes a quick trip across the tracks to the seedy side of town." He sighed. "But, we'll

stick the kids on the back burner for now until we see how
the others play out."

"Agreed. So who else have we got?" Kevin scanned the
file again. "Okay, there were two brothers-in-law, Mortimer
and Justin. And two grown nephews, Robert Wainsborough
and Timothy Knowles." He glanced at Pete. "How much
do you suppose the nephews were left in the will? Enough
to make murder look profitable?"

"It doesn't take much, councilor, believe me. I once
had a case where a man killed his friend over a crab cake.
Some people are nothing but greedy bastards." Pete sighed
again and got to his feet. "Well, I'll check out these folks
and get back to you."

"Better check out my client, too," Kevin told him.
"The guy says he's innocent, and I think I believe him. But
it'd be nice to know for sure, so I don't end up looking like
a fool."

Pete laughed. "You mean attorneys don't try to look
like fools on purpose? That's how Matlock does it. It always
works for him."

Kevin sighed. "Life should be so easy."

CHAPTER 3

June 2000:

As Pete typed up the report of his investigation, he could only shake his head and laugh. He'd been right when he told the attorney that some people were nothing but greedy bastards. And the Knowles family seemed to have more than their fair share. Any one of them could have bumped off the old lady for pocket change without blinking an eyelash...well, except maybe for her son. Brian Knowles had always defended his mother against everyone, including his wife. And when Pete had attended Charlotte's funeral last February, Brian had seemed sincerely broken up about his mother's murder. Tears of grief had streamed down his face, and it looked like he hadn't slept since her death. While it was true that grief could be faked, Pete hadn't gotten the impression Brian was faking. The only time Brian had ever defied his mother was over marrying Gwen. Charlotte had not approved of her, but Brian had married her anyway. Still, Pete decided, Brian could go on the back burner with his kids. For now.

Gwen, on the other hand...Pete shook his head again and typed up what he'd learned about Gwendolyn Harmon Knowles.

June 1975:

Gwen never felt she belonged in the Boston-Irish-Catholic, working-class community where she grew up—seven siblings and her parents Joseph and Kathleen Harmon all crammed into one little two-bedroom house. Gwen always felt she was so much better than everyone around her. In actuality, she hated where she was and felt she'd eventually suffocate if she didn't get away from the bad smells permeating the tiny place.

She hated her shabby surroundings. And when she thought the family's struggles couldn't get worse, they did—her alcoholic father left the household and disappeared. They couldn't locate him. In order to make it without his financial help—not that it had ever been all that much, for he wasted a considerable portion of his meat plant wages on drink—the family went on public assistance, and every child old enough had to work. Gwen resented everything about growing up poor. The used clothing she and her siblings wore embarrassed her. As did the taunts, "You stink! You need to take a bath!" and the humiliating government hand-outs that included that awful-tasting cheese. She had felt her face getting red hot every time she walked into a soup kitchen with her mother and siblings. The humiliation just didn't stop!

Gwen felt sorry for her mother, seeing the burden that raising her and her sibling, alone and with so little, posed for her. Her mother was overwhelmed and nothing had ever been right or normal. So some household chores didn't get done or were not kept up as they could have been. Gwen and her siblings did as much as could as they could to help around the house, but it was never enough.

Gwen remembered when she had purchased some Easter chicks with her babysitting money. She'd been overjoyed to have the fluffy little creatures, so soft and warm and sweet. She put the pretty, little birds on a towel in a cardboard box and placed chicken food in it, so they'd be fed, warm, and cozy. The next morning she couldn't wait to go to the cellar to see them.

Why are they so quiet, she wondered, staring anxiously at their box on the cellar floor. *Yesterday, I couldn't get them to shut up.*

Nervously she lifted the towel she'd put over the cardboard box the night before. "Oh, no! My chicks are dead!" she cried, picking up a pale yellow feather with a couple drops of red on the end. She sank down on the cellar steps, heartbroken and crying, with tears streaming down her face and the feather clutched in her hand. Rats had gotten to her pretty little chicks and killed them all.

Rats! Why did God have to make rats? She despised them and wished they'd all die! Her family only had to deal with rats in the cellar because they were so poor. She *hated* being poor—even worse than she hated the rats.

Because of all she'd endured, Gwen had developed a very determined spirit. "Someday, I will get rich and never be poor again!" she often said, especially when something happened that brought home the message that she was a victim of poverty. Early in her life, she made up her mind to use everything she could, inside of her or outside, to rise above her circumstances.

In a fantasy she created, she'd be a member of high society one day. And her children would never suffer what she had...

"Hey there, you okay?" Father Michael Branigan asked, helping her up off the ground.

Embarrassed, Gwen looked up at the young minister of their Mother of Sorrows Church. She'd been walking home that evening from her after-school job at McDonalds, a good distance from where she lived, and she'd slipped on the icy pavement.

"Let me help you up, young lady," the handsome, young priest said, smiling and offering his hand.

She nodded, yes and gave him her arm.

He prevented a second fall, when she slipped again, and caught her by the arm. "You could use hot chocolate. You're all wet and freezing. It's okay. Ya know I know your mother and family."

Seeing no reason to distrust Father Branigan, Gwen happily agreed, and the two carefully walked down the icy streets to the minister's church apartment.

Gwen had telephoned her mother and had just put down the phone when Father Branigan called her name, saying he had a wall picture he wanted to show her. When she found the bedroom he was in, he met her at the door— naked. Shocked and fearful, she backed away, but not in time. He pulled her to him and then threw her onto his bed. Frightened and crying, she pleaded and struggled to get free. He began kissing her forcefully. Then suddenly, he stopped pulled away, and ejaculated on her plaid, wool skirt. Apologizing fiercely, he rose to leave, saying he'd get towel and clean her skirt.

She'd never told a soul, keeping the guilt and shame to herself. Her mother was already in over her head, raising the large family single-handedly. And telling her about the incident would only press her down further. She was almost lethargic most of the time even dealing with the few things she did. She kept the household going, but just barely. Gwen worried that it wouldn't take much more and her mother might snap. Moreover, the church protected the family. It was all they had to cling to for their very lives and to keep them from total despair. Gwen couldn't take that out from under them.

But that incident with Father Branigan added to her feelings of contempt. Even the Catholic Church was filthy and dirty. Everything in her surroundings was ugly and disgusting. Her mind was made up, she was going to get as far away from there as she could and was never looking back!

She studied hard throughout school, thinking she'd get a scholarship to college and a better life. Lucky for her, her hopes were answered when she graduated from high school and received a full scholarship to Dartmouth College.

Brian Knowles was another gift. When she'd met the handsome young man on campus the autumn of her sophomore year, she saw her future looking up more than she had anticipated. From a wealthy, elevated Briarton, Connecticut, family, Brian was studying for his graduate degree in Advertising and Communications—Gwen's own major.

On a marvelous autumn afternoon, Brian pulled up in front of her dorm in his new Porshe. "Get in here, you lovely thing you," he told her, smilingly, as he jumped from the car and ran around to her side. He gathered her in his arms and kissed her deeply then proposed. She felt the sun shining on her, magically, as if she were living in a fairytale.

October 1999:

"That girl Gwen hired won't cut the mustard. She has to go, Brian," Charlotte announced, talking about the new employee of Brian and Gwen's advertising firm.

Buttin' in again! Gwen thought angrily, as she ease-dropped on Brian's phone conversation from an extension in the outer office. *She's always making decisions for us.*"

Her mother-in-law was correct that their new employee wasn't working out. Nonetheless, Gwen resented Charlotte's interference. Gwen had hired the girl, and *she* should be the one to decide if the bitch had to go.

"Um-mm," Brian mumbled in agreement. He wasn't one to argue, especially with his mother—or his wife.

Everything would have been perfect if only Gwen didn't have Charlotte as her mother-in-law. She hated the fact that she could never measure up to Charlotte's expectations. Brian's mother was the one thing keeping Gwen from having everything the way she wanted it, completely. And Charlotte's meddling had only gotten worse once their two children became teenagers.

Gwen knew she was a good mother, better than Charlotte had been for Brian. But Charlotte was always criticizing her and usurping her authority, both at home and at the business. *That bitch!*

"Brian, your mother runs the business, our household, Alfred and Jessica, everything," Gwen snarled once he was off the phone. "She's been interfering in our lives since we met. I'm sick of it! When are you going to say something to her? She's your mother!"

"Mother's only trying to help!"

Gwen snorted. *Like hell!* Charlotte had never forgiven Gwen for winning Brian's heart and his hand in marriage. No, the old bitty had picked out some high-society princess for her precious son, and she was totally stunned when Brian had insisted on marrying Gwen. As far as Gwen knew, it was the only time he'd ever defied the old gal. But Charlotte had made Gwen pay for it over the years. Oh, yes. Her snide comments and outright digs always served to put Gwen in her place—the poor relation, the socially-unacceptable daughter-in-law she was ashamed to admit to. Charlotte made no secret of how she felt about Gwen. Gwen's only consolation was that she hadn't been able to convince Brian to divorce her. Yet.

Her own mother never interfered. Gwen had been supporting her mother since her marriage to Brian, and her generosity had elevated her mother's status immensely. Now she lived in one of Briarton's nicer neighborhoods and had everything she needed to live comfortably. Gwen allowed the children to spend time with both their grandmothers, yet thinking about their safety gave her pause. When it came to Alfred and Jessica, she was a little overprotective. Perhaps she strove harder than most mothers to protect them because of what she'd experienced as a young girl with the priest.

Brian's defense of his mother only increased the resentment swirling around in Gwen's mind. It angered her to think that after she'd had to go through all that she had while growing up and clawing her way out of that pit to a prosperous life, everything still wasn't hers to have and hold. And, when she said everything, she meant *everything!*

CHAPTER 4

June 2000:

Pete sighed. Yes, Gwen had an excellent motive to kill her mother-in-law, but she also had an ironclad alibi. She'd been at a party when Charlotte Knowles died, and there were nearly fifty witnesses to prove it. Pete put his report on Gwen in the file and moved on to Timothy. Tim was a weird duck, Pete mused, but perhaps he had good reason to be...

Timothy Knowles had kept a dark secret all of his life. To the public, the son of Briarton patriarch Justin Knowles seemed self-assured. Nothing could be farther from the truth.

When not heavily using marijuana, cocaine, meth, oxycontin, heroin, alcohol, and any other mind-altering drugs he could get his hands on, Timothy lacked confidence to the point of being nervous and jittery. And on account of his low self-esteem, he also indulged in an addiction to prostitutes.

The young, unmarried accountant had had concerns about his manhood since his childhood. He'd heard the whispers about his Uncle Mortimer's homosexuality and walked around fearful that he might have the weakness circling inside of him. And then something dreadful happened when he was fourteen years old.

August 1980:

His father took his young family to Martha's Vineyard as he often did in the summer. Timothy and two of the boys were rooming next door to their parents. Timothy had just gone outside in the moonlight for a solitary stroll. A middle-aged man the family had met in the restaurant was also out walking. Tim recalled how friendly the tall, bulky man had been toward the whole family throughout the five days they'd been at the lodge. He'd expressed how much he missed his wife that he lost to cancer a year ago. The man poured out his heart to the family. Tim's mother, a deeply sympathetic type, had shed tears listening to the sad widower. Even his father had shown compassion toward the stranger.

That night, as Tim walked along the beach, the man he'd felt comfortable with earlier that day called out to him.

"Hello, young fellow. Goin' fer a wac, huh?" The successful businessman had a powerfully thick upper New England accent.

Tim smiled and replied that he was. The gentleman then asked if he could join him. Tim could see no reason to refuse. As a matter of fact, he thought that a stroll along the beach with the older man might be enjoyable. The moon shed a shaft of dim light on them as they engaged in conversation. Tim talked about school, and the well-traveled man talked about the different places he'd been.

As he and the older man approached an area isolated by darkness, the man grabbed Tim. He was big-boned as well as tall, while Tim was slender, though above average in height.

"What are you doing?" Tim screamed in fear.

The man told him he wanted to have sex with him. And with that, he threw Tim down against the pebbly ground. Tim struggled, to no avail. The man's hard fist slammed into his temple. Everything went black.

When he regained consciousness, Tim pleaded through his fear and disgust. "Please, just let me go. I promise not to say anything to anyone."

Nonetheless, the lust-driven man continued his assault, hitting Tim about his face and head. Tim finally managed to knee the man in the groin. He broke away and took off.

The man chased him, but Tim was young and quick and he outran the older man.

Before long, he'd reached the lodge and was breathlessly telling his parents about the near rape. His parents notified the police.

The man immediately took off in his car. But he didn't get far before police arrested him.

This incident planted seeds of doubt that made Tim question his sexuality. He wondered if he'd sent subtle or unconscious signals that had caused the man to make a move on him.

"I don't think I'm effeminate," he worriedly assured himself. "What could have provoked that guy? I've heard other guys say men came onto them. But it's never happened to me before or since." His mind turned over and over with questions until Tim decided to double-check himself for any hints that his appearance or characteristics had invited the man's attentions. But he could find no reason for the attack, which made him feel a little better, although it did not completely allay his fears.

While in his junior year of college, he met Jasmine Smith. He knew the first time he saw her that it was love at first sight. His first love. Tim found Jasmine's spirit remarkable and redeeming. She was different from any woman he'd ever known. She was beautiful and brilliant, and she affected him as no other woman had. She was tall, around five-feet-eleven and willowy. Her complexion was nut brown and smooth as silk. She wore her long, black hair in a ponytail. Her eyes, the most compelling part of her looks, were dark brown with thick, long, dark lashes. And she had lovely, inviting lips.

"You're a new student here, aren't you? Until today I've never seen you." Tim said with a smile as he caught up with the pretty African American girl on campus. Jasmine was a new freshman student at the very pricey private college. She was one of seven minority students, all of them on a financially-sponsored scholarships.

"You haven't seen me around because I'm a freshman," Jasmine replied, smiling.

Wow! And on top of everything she has the softest, sweetest voice, he thought, thoroughly drawn to her. Tim was hooked from that very day. The two young people began seeing each other for dates to the movies and strolls on campus. It was a hopeful period. One would never know by her pleasant personality that she had lived all her life doing without the things Tim took for granted.

Jasmine had experienced tough times growing up. Her family was extremely poor. Her father, Harold Smith, was often out of work and could barely support himself, his wife, and their five children.

Jasmine idolized her handsome young father. And his daughter had a special place in his heart as well. It seems that everyone who knew Harold liked him. This was especially so with women. His looks attracted women like flies at a picnic. And it was his nature to mingle with the people in the community.

During Jasmine's sophomore year something terrible happened to her father, and all of a sudden the young girl's life became the worst it could ever be.

"Daddy, daddy, please don't die! Please, please don't leave me!" Jasmine cried hysterically as her father lay dying on the ground. He'd been shot by a jealous husband. The ambulance pulled up too late, and Harold had died in his daughter's arms.

The tragic incident was too much for Jasmine's mother, thirty-seven-year-old Barbara Smith. She lost her mind and ended up in a psychiatric hospital. Jasmine was forced to leave school to support her siblings. Tim soon lost track of her.

In later years, Tim became involved with many women. As a matter of fact, a couple of those almost pulled him into marriage. But he never got over his self-doubts. And he never got over Jasmine.

May 1996:

"Okay, now who is this dude I'm supposed to meet for the coke?" Tim asked himself looking around in the darkness of the dimly-lit nightclub. His usual supplier was in jail, but Tim needed something, and needed it bad. A disc jockey was blasting hip hop and rap music, entertaining the mostly Black crowd. Some couples were on the dance floor, dancing.

Tim stood in the shadows near the bar, waiting for someone by the name of Matt who was supposed to come up to him. In all of his years, he'd never even been to Briarton's lower end, and he felt uncomfortable. Even when he and Jasmine Smith dated, he never went to her family's house.

"Coming to my house might not be a good thing," she'd told him, explaining about how risky the environment was. Violence could break out in her neighborhood at any time.

Going by the number of people here, on a Thursday night, the club was popular. He'd just headed for the bar when a tall young black man approached. "You lookin' for me? Your name Brad?"

"If you're Matt," Tim nervously replied. It wasn't just the drug deal, the whole scene intimidated him.

"Look, I'm givin' you my house address. You can come there anytime and get what you need from me. In the meantime, I'm givin' you somethin' now," he said and reached out to Tim, handing him three small packets. He also handed him a slip of paper with an address on it. "It should last you a while."

Tim unobtrusively placed some bills in his hand.

Matt counted the money. "I'm outta here. See you when you need me."

Just as the drug dealer was turning to leave, a woman's voice broke through the noisy surroundings.

"I ain't drunk! I'm goin' home. All yall kin go to hell!"

The woman causing the commotion triggered something in Tim when he looked in her direction. He thought that it couldn't be who he thought it was and strained to see her more clearly across the darkened room.

"Uh, okay, I'll be in touch," Tim said to Matt, his eyes trained on the woman.

"Hey, man, that ain't nobody but Jasmine. She'll give you a good trick, cheap. Hey. Later!" and with that, Matt was on his way out of the nightclub.

Hearing the name, Tim decided it must be his Jasmine after all. He'd have to help her. His heart pounded like a drum as he crossed the room to her.

"Jasmine, it's Tim. Timothy Knowles from university."

Would she remember him? He was almost shaking with nerves. She was someone he'd once loved deeply. No one had come close to making him feel the way he had about her. He was shattered when she left school. He'd prayed that she would turn up in his life again. He even tried to find her, but he'd never known where to go look.

"Yeah, I remember you. Timothy Knowles! After all these years! How could I not remember you? You and me used to date even though we was as different as…as the light of day and darkness." She was thoroughly drunk and slurring her words. She tried to rise from the barstool and would have fallen to the floor if Tim hadn't caught her elbow.

"Whoa! I've got you!" he said. "Come on show me where you live. I'm taking you home." With her hanging onto his shoulder and his arm around her waist, he guided her out of the nightclub.

"Ju—just down the street. A couple houses down the stre—streets," she muttered, almost collapsing against him. Soon they were in front of a grouping of small, wood frame houses. "Here we go, this is it! Ain't much, but this is where I lay my head," she said with a laugh

Timothy didn't laugh though. Seeing her drunk disappointed him. She looked the same, although tiredness edged her pretty face. It was evident that she'd had a rough time of it.

"Where's the, the key?" She reached inside her large pocketbook. "Hell, I can't find nothin' in here. You look!" And she handed him the purse.

He fished around inside it and finally came up with the key. As they went inside, he found a switch near the front door and turned a light on the tiny, almost barren surroundings.

"Timothy, this is what I call home. Whadaya think? Surely not the mansion you grew up in, huh?"

"Let's get you to bed. Okay?" Still holding her up, he looked around at the two doors, trying to guess which one was her bedroom.

"That one!" she told him, pointing. He picked her up, and she broke into laughter. "Oh boy! This might be fun."

Inside the room he laid her down on the unmade bed, covered her with the sheet and a blanket.

"I'm leaving and you are going to get some sleep," he said sternly, feeling like a parent.

She sat up, gathering herself. "D' ya know what I am? 'Like my drunken de—ceased—father. Did—did—you—

know wha—hap—pened—ta him? Died in my—arms.
Dead as—a—doorknob. Hey! Don't you want ta—slee—
p—with me? What are you? Are—are you—gay or—
somethin'?"

Sleep and drunkenness must have overpowered her,
for she fell back on the bed and was instantly asleep. It was
extremely painful, after all the years he yearned to be with
her again, to discover she was a whore and a drunk, but her
words had also cast doubt on his manhood.

She was snoring when he left house and stepped
outside into the dark deserted night. Not only was he
reacting to the pain of seeing Jasmine in her condition, but
his already shaken self-image had just been rattled a little
more.

CHAPTER 5

June 2000:

It was clear that Tim had a number of problems, Pete mused, and no alibi to speak of. He'd told police he wasn't feeling well and had been at home alone and in bed when his aunt was murdered. But Pete couldn't find a solid motive either. The amount Tim would inherit from Charlotte's estate would be a nice windfall, but there was no evidence that he needed the money. Nor did it appear that he had any particular axe to grind with her. No, other than the lack of a verified alibi, Tim seemed to be in the clear.

Pete finished typing the report on Tim, printed it out, and set it the file with the others. Who was next? he wondered as he looked through his notes. Ah, yes. Charlotte's brother-in-law, Justin Knowles...

August 1999:

Seventy-year-old Justin struggled to bring his thoughts to the subject at hand. He had come to the board meeting after spending the day with his tall, blond, and lovely young mistress in her trailer in nearby Bedbury. She was a manicurist and worked in the salon where his wife Claire got her nails done. Justin felt his skin prickle just thinking about her.

Suddenly startled out of his lascivious thoughts by something one of the board members said, Justin surged to his feet. "That's a ridiculous move!" Standing at the head of the table surrounded by the twelve board members, he shook his fist for emphasis. "St. John Methodist stands on tradition. Paul's recommendation goes against everything this college stands for."

He glared at Paul Anderson, the school's president, then scanned the reactions of the other board members hoping to see his own outrage on their faces. After all, liberal-leaning fifty-five-year-old Anderson had just proposed changing the Spring Arts presentation from classical to contemporary music. The idea was simply unthinkable.

"We're in the twenty-first century now, and the school is ready for a change," Anderson said, rising also. "The Arts and Music departments and I are looking at the idea of bringing in Porter, Bernstein, Gershwin and some of the more modern composers this year."

"St John has its classical integrity to uphold," Justin responded. By now he was totally into the heated debate and had forgotten about the fun time with his mistress. He wanted to play the role of the powerful overseer. It was his duty. After all the Knowles' legacy could never be taken lightly. His wealthy banking family was at the top of the social ladder, even venerated in Briarton, as the statues and stone memorials, busts and portraits all around the city clearly showed. His family had founded St. John Methodist College. Hell, his ancestors had helped establish America. He was *important*, damn it.

So why hadn't the board listened to him? Stunned, he slumped in his chair as the board voted to change the spring program to a more modern style of music.

September 1999:

Justin had his family surrounding him as he cooked steaks on the grill in the massive backyard of the family's estate. Timothy and Claire all sat around the long picnic table on this warm summer day.

"A trust has been handed down, son," Justin told Tim. "You have the responsibility to uphold the respectability and principles passed down by generations of 'Knowles.'"

Justin rose from the table to go check on his steaks. His cell phone rang, and he reached into his pocket. "Yes,

I've been waiting for your call," he said, walking out of ear shot. "I'll be there, zappo! Yes, sweet thing! Can't wait!"

When he returned to his family ,he said, "Tim, finish the steaks. I have to leave right away on some business."

"But, Justin, it's a Saturday. Can't it wait?" Claire whined.

He pulled off his apron. "I'm sorry, Claire. It's an emergency. I have no choice. I'll be back as soon as I can." He gave her an absent-minded kiss on the cheek and ran for his car.

His mind swirled with what was waiting for him. He could feel his mistress's trailer shaking, rattling, and rolling. That's what it felt like when he was with her. She had captivated him from the first time he spotted her at an annual Briarton Fourth of July celebration. She was one of the hostesses, usually chosen because they were young, blond, and gorgeous. Hostesses passed out programs for the event. When the most beautiful of all the young women with a program came up to him, he leaned over and whispered in her ear, "You knock me over, you gorgeous thing, you." He told her to put her phone number on a program and give it to him. "I'll take you out for the time of your life," he whispered, more captivated than he'd ever been.

Everything about him sent the message there could be a lot in it for her if she complied, and she had.

June 2000:

Pete typed the report on Justin with mixed feelings. The old man had nothing to gain, at least monetarily, from his sister-in-law's death, but what about other motives? Had Charlotte known about Justin's mistress, Sharon Wilson? Would he have for his pride? It was clear the Knowles' good name was of paramount importance to him, but how far would he go to protect it. Pete sighed in frustration. He'd found no evidence that Charlotte had known about Sharon or that she would have told anyone if she had. From all appearances, Charlotte was just as protective of the family's reputation as Justin was, so there was no proof she would have been a threat.

But what about Justin's wife, Claire Winston Knowles?

At sixty-seven, tall, slender Claire was still quite an attractive brunette. She was a blue-blood through and through, a wife well-suited for Justin Knowles. Tepid and eager to please, she geared all of her resources toward her husband, her children, and toward maintaining the elevated life she'd always known.

Claire and Justin shared the same heritage. She was descended from James Rutherford who became a wealthy textile mill owner. He was among the earliest groups to arrive from England to establish the American colonies. The Knowles family had also arrived with the Mayflower. The wealthy aristocrats owned plantations operating in the south and also did some slave trading.

Claire had always known about her husband's dalliances. They had gone on throughout their long marriage. But realizing she had everything to lose and nothing to gain, the high-bred Claire looked the other way.

Pete could find nothing in Claire's background or recent behavior that suggested she had anything to gain by killing her sister-in-law, unless Charlotte had threatened to spill the beans on Justin's many affairs. But there was no proof that the decedent even knew.

He moved onto to Justin's mistress, Sharon Wilson. Although highly unlikely, it was at least possible that she had a motive to kill the old lady—but again, only if Charlotte knew about her affair with Justin—an affair that from what Pete could see would soon be over anyway...

Sharon was a carefree spirit, even though she'd grown up in one of Briarton's poorer working class neighborhoods. She was endowed with unusual beauty, and girls in the neighborhood often picked fights with her and her sisters because they were tall, slender and shapely, with great complexions, exquisite features, lustrous, long hair, and fantastic light eyes. The community Sharon grew up in left much to be desired, and she used to imagine having a fairytale life. She was restless and yearned to go places, meet new people, and live life with abandon.

Life was rough and although she and her family lacked a great deal, Sharon used her ingenuity to make things better. Like when she discovered she had a talent for sewing. Using her mother's second-hand sewing machine and material she bought at fabric discount centers, she sewed beautiful outfits for herself and her siblings.

The clothes and her extraordinary looks made her a real "knock out." Later, as she became a young woman, she participated in local beauty pageants and won several. In fact, it was while she was competing in a beauty contest that she encountered Bill Morrison, a city-slick black man who promised he would manage her "call girl" experience.

A natural dreamer, Sharon was inspired by all aspects in her surroundings. She imagined a stairway to heaven, and bright sunlight seemed to lead her to green pastures and flowery pathways. Her childhood was played out through hopes, dreams, and aspirations. On her family's rare day trip to the beach her heart swelled with longing as she gazed at people on the balconies and terraces of the luxurious hotels. It was a life-style she and her family would never have but that didn't stop her from having dreams.

She often pretended her tiny street was a canal in Venice or Holland. Once, around the time of Good Friday, her narrow street became the place for Christ's Resurrection. She'd swear that dark clouds and the Crucifixion appeared there. And brilliant sunshine poured into the tiny lane on the day Christ rose.

Her father, Reverend Donald Wilson was an uneducated, self-made preacher. He held his church services for a small group of congregants in a storefront in the community. As storefront churches are known to do, his ministry suffered financially, but his fiery sermons, along with the tambourines and shouting, set the tiny storefront service ablaze.

When he wasn't preaching, he salvaged furniture, clothing—anything tossed out on the street—and hauled it to the junk dealers in his dilapidated old truck. His children also collected things people no longer wanted: newspapers, soda bottles, and clothing.

"I used my brother's wagon to transport the items to junk," When talking about her rough upbringing, Sharon was known to remark, "My mother, bless her heart, worked hard at a local factory. But we survived, barely."

June 2000:

Pete wondered if Sharon had told Justin that since the age of nineteen she'd used prostitution to raise her standard of living. He supposed it didn't matter anymore. According to her, she'd found true love and her affair with Justin was over.

Pete just hoped Justin didn't suffer a heart attack when she told him.

CHAPTER 6

Pete got himself a beer and studied what he'd done so far. None of the suspects so far looked very promising. But there was still Charlotte's nephew Robert Wainsborough...

Robert grew up in New York City society in a brownstone mansion. But his social history began in Philadelphia. His grandfather prompted cornerstone and hallmark edifices and masterful works of architecture around the Quaker City.

The Knowles, Hornsbys, Wainsboroughs belonged to that group of old and nouveau rich New England and East Coast famous families. They were invited to the compounds of the worlds' richest, the Vanderbilts, Rockefellers, the Duponts, The Rothchilds and the Roosevelts, and others famous in industry, business, politics and finance.

Single, handsome, thirty-two-year-old Robert lived in a pent house apartment in Manhattan. He owned a small, used book store on the Upper-East side that specialized in collectibles and antique books and was fairly successful.

His family and his Aunt Charlotte, his father's sister, had close ties. He and his sister and brother had great times with their Aunt Charlotte, Uncle Wallace and Cousin Brian at the Briarton mansion.

June 2000:

Robert *appeared* to have been devoted to his aunt, and he was wealthy in his own right. Pete couldn't see that the man had anything to gain by Charlotte's death. He did have a girlfriend, but it was unlikely she had any motive for the murder. Pete shrugged and picked up his notes on Marcia Ramsey...

July 1997:

Vacationing at the New Jersey shore, twenty-four-year-old Marcia had awakened before dawn, gathered her easel and paints, and made the short walk down to a special spot. She was alone in the beautiful, serene, quiet, and familiar surroundings. She sighed with how peaceful she felt. She couldn't remember the Delaware Bay ever being this enchanting. Her mind wandered back to her childhood and the carefree, happy summers she and her family spent there.

She put down her equipment in a place where tall grass bordered the shoreline. It was an area with which she was very familiar. Some of her happiest memories were of a spot near a wooden pier. She and the other children had frolicked and swam there for hours on end. Over the summers they formed and reformed friendships. Time stood still for them and their families at the bayside resort. At the end of a carefree day, when darkness was encroaching and night transferred a blanket of the dark, magical, mystical universe, they were partakers of 'the good life.'

"Who's that?" Marcia asked herself as she looked up from her easel. Putting down her brush and straining her eyes, she thought she saw a tall, handsome stranger. And then, as suddenly as he'd appeared, the man vanished. He reminded her of when she was a teen and a handsome boy had seized her attention. He seemed attracted her as well but too shy to do anything about it.

Marcia wondered why that handsome boy from long ago still haunted her. It wasn't only that she had dreams about him, but he came into her thoughts regularly. On the rare occasion she ran into him, or happened to spot him her heart raced with joy.

Like the time she was driving down Route 222, and a car, a black Escalade was in the lane beside hers. She was trying to figure out why the handsome man behind the wheel was familiar and appealing, when his car moved ahead and was soon out of sight.

"I've seen that man somewhere," she said to herself. It occurred to her where she'd spotted him. It was in Macy's in downtown Philadelphia. She was on the opposite side of the store when her eye caught sight of him and his young pretty wife. He was pushing a stroller with a cute baby, likely a boy. And then her mind carried her back in time to when she was a teenager and saw him that summer at the New Jersey resort. "Is he that person?" Nodding, she answered herself "That's him. He's the one." At both sightings it seemed he hadn't seen her. Someone told her his name was Kevin, but she wondered if she'd ever find out for sure.

November 1999:

At twenty-seven Marcia was definitely at a low point. Her advertising business in Manhattan had been going strong. And then September 11, 2001, America's worst tragedy happened, and her business took a hit. Anthony Brookins, her boyfriend since childhood informed her they were finished. He'd dropped her and was seeing her first cousin, Debra Woodruff.

Her mother's niece had never been principled or concerned about others. In actuality she was ruthless! And regrettably, Marcia and her cousin could have been sisters, look-a-like sisters.

Many times they'd been mistaken for each other. Even relatives, until they were up close enough to see the differences, got the two mixed up. And so, while she was heartbroken because she'd been in love with Anthony since they were kids, she wasn't surprised when he informed her that they were finished and that he and Debra were seeing each other.

Marcia decided to pull into a diner turnpike while traveling back to Philadelphia from visiting friends in New Jersey. She sat at one of the empty small tables and ordered lunch. Her head swam with the many depressing issues in her life, and she almost didn't notice when a handsome man approached with a tray.

"Is anyone sitting here?" he asked with a smile. "If not, lunch would taste a lot better if I could join you."

He was so tall and handsome, and his manner so friendly, it was difficult for Marcia to refuse. "Uh, sure—I mean you're welcomed to sit here."

"Robert Wainsborough," he said holding out his hand.

"Marcia Ramsey," she responded as she shook hands with him.

As their conversation progressed, they discovered they had a great deal in common, and lunch lasted for hours instead of the few minutes Marcia had expected it to. As she and Robert got to know each other, a spontaneous friendship began, and from there, Marcia hoped, much, much more would develop.

May 2000:

"Wow!" Marcia couldn't help being impressed, seeing the elegant surroundings, as she and Robert entered the long driveway at his grandparents lovely Mainline home. It was late-spring. Gladiolas, azaleas, and other lovely flowers stretched all around the massive house. A kind of magical enchantment seemed settled over the luscious grounds of the property. *So this is how they really live,* she thought, seeing the dimension of wealth and status that even out-performed what she was used to.

She felt incredible warmth and acceptance when Robert's handsome, aristocratic grandparents invited them in through the wide double doors.

June 2000:

"Robert's not making this kind of living out of a used book store," Pete muttered. "But then, he hardly needs to. He comes from a stinking rich family. And while the woman, Marcia, isn't as wealthy, she ain't that poor, either.

What Marcia really wants is a man to love her, and killing Robert's aunt would not help her there at all. What possible could either he or Marcia have for the murder?"

Discouraged at the possibility he might never uncover the murderer, Pete turned to the next name on the list.

CHAPTER 7

As he picked up the next stack of notes, Pete thought about the long conversation he'd had with Mortimer Knowles. The interview hadn't gone nearly as Pete had expected. Mortimer had needed someone to talk to, and as Pete took copious notes, the man had confessed—but not to the crime Pete had wanted him to...

Mortimer had handed Pete a beer and cleared his throat. "Well, sir, you see, sir, me and my father did a terrible thing back in 1953...

October 1953:

Dark, eerie shadows invaded the barn and woods. Mortimer and his father, John Knowles, had prepared a hangman's noose the day before and were waiting inside the barn for Arthur Besselman to show up. Soon they heard his new 1953 Pontiac pulling up outside.

"Get the cover over this thing, fast!" his father ordered.

Mortimer said nothing. He grabbed the blanket and threw it over the set-up they would use to kill the man. Then they waited for the agent to get out of his car.

Smiling and arrogant, as he always was, Besselman entered the barn, carrying his leather black satchel. "Good evening, gentlemen."

John grabbed his arm, twisting it behind his back and rendering him helpless.

"What, what you doing?" Besselman cried. "Stop it! Stop it! I won't ask for more money!"

They ignored his pleas.

"Toss me the rope!" John told his son.

Mortimer did as ordered. John tried to put the looped rope around Besselman's neck, but he was struggling too much. Realizing the trouble his father was having, Mortimer climbed down to help. The men subdued Bessleman, drug him up to the hayloft, and slipped the rope around his neck. Throughout the ordeal the two men seemed deaf to Besselman's pleas. They threw him off the second floor loft, and the rope put an end to his life.

June 2000:

Mortimer had been plagued by the same nightmare over and over again and would wake, sweating and shaking, in his tiny, dingy room at the bowery in New York City.

"It just won't stop!" he told Pete miserably. "I'll never get away from it. It keeps coming back, just the way it went that evening." He pulled out the bottle he relied on to blot out the horrible incident from his memory.

"'I neet more money for m'self,' Besselman would tell my father. 'Dis ese not easy, Vhat I do. You don't vant no one to know vhat you do, do you?' Besselman strung my father along for years. 'The sleazy German has run this ransom for silence into the ground,' my father told me, burning with anger after the many years of being blackmailed. 'Besselman must be eliminated.'"

"What did this man have on your father?" Pete asked.

"Besselman was his link to an Aryan group that promoted racism in Europe. My father hired Besselman to transfer large sums of money and secret information between Europe—mainly Germany—and the United States."

A murderer is a murderer, Peter thought now. But try as he might, he could find no connection between what Mortimer told him and the death of Charlotte Knowles.

He printed out his report on Mortimer. He'd pass the information along to Kevin and let him decide what to do with it.

CHAPTER 8

December, 2000:

The Charlotte Knowles murder trial was one of the most publicized New England had ever seen. Perhaps only the Lizzie Borden trial had drawn more attention.

The courtroom was typical of the sort you find in small, old-fashioned, New England towns. In the compact courtroom, Reporters took rapid notes, recorders were running, and cameras were aimed at the witness box.

"Court is in session." announced the bailiff.

Silence fell over the eager, chatty crowd.

Kevin looked over at his client. Matt's eyes had lost none of their hopelessness. Kevin could relate. During the two weeks since the trial began, the only time Kevin had had a reason to smile was after he'd returned to the courtroom following a phone conversation during recess with his son, Junior, and his mother-in-law who was taking care of him while Kevin worked.

Still, he had to keep Matt's spirits up or the man would be useless in testifying for his own defense.

Disbelief and confusion shrouded Cook's dark-skinned face. From time to time he shook his head in response to a question. Tall and slender, Cook appeared younger than his thirty years. He was clearly nice-looking, and for someone who had begun abusing drugs at age thirteen he could have looked a whole lot worse.

Kevin leaned over and placed his hand on top of Matthew Cook's trembling one. "Things are not as grim as they seem. Just stay calm and tell the jury the truth."

The bailiff called Matt's name. He rose from his seat and headed for the front of the courtroom to take the stand.

The prosecutor, forty-year-old John Goodman, brushed back his red hair from his forehead as Matt approached. Goodman's sparkling eyes and bright smile said he relished the opportunity to cross examine the defendant. Goodman had recently won an important case involving six young black males who'd killed a white man in a restaurant parking lot during a robbery, and that had apparently bolstered his confidence.

Kevin took Matt through his normal daily life and then his actions on the day Charlotte Knowles was murdered. He encouraged him to expound on his alibi, such as it was. But eventually, he had to give the floor to Goodman for his cross-examination.

"Matthew Cook, did you sell drugs in Briarton?" Goodman demanded, surging to his feet.

The defendant nodded, and softly answered, "Yes."

"You sold drugs for quite some time, I take it?" Goodman paused for a moment to let Matt nod in response. "Things began to get a little rough," the prosecutor continued, "Business started to dry up and you needed money for more drugs. You had a big drug habit, right?"

"Your Honor, I object," Kevin declared, rising as he spoke. "Whether or not my client has a drug addiction does not make him a murderer!"

"Overruled. The defendant will answer the question."

"No, sir, I don't have no drug habit," Matt replied solemnly.

"You needed money and so on the evening of February fourteen, two-thousand, you went to the home of Charlotte Hornsby Wainsborough Knowles."

No, Matt, don't squirm up there for God's sake, Kevin silently commanded his client. *It makes the jury think you're guilty.*

"Was the gun one you stole or one you purchased?" Goodman demanded. "Did you have a license for it? You found the victim in the kitchen, used the gun you carried there, and shot her to death. You then grabbed her valuables and money, and left the house."

The courtroom was so quiet Kevin could swear he heard Matt's heart pounding in fear. Or maybe it was his heart and not Matt's he was hearing.

"Aunt Charlotte was always my favorite of my father's sisters," Robert whispered to Marcia as they watched the defense attorney whisper to his client. "She was so easy to like. I used to visit her when I was young, and she spared no expense to make it a fun time for us kids. I can't stand to look at that creep sitting up there. I hope they throw the book at that black murderer."

Marcia barely heard a word he said. She was fixated on the attorney seated with Matthew Cook.

That's him! That's him! She couldn't believe she was looking at was the very man who'd stayed in her memory, that she'd had those chance encounters with. Realizing that her face might reveal how excited she was, she tried to rein in her emotions. "Uh, yes, that guy should have the book thrown at him."

Kevin lay awake, unable to unwind from the day's intense courtroom activity. However, he also thought a lot about the woman he'd seen in the audience. He'd seen her before a few times, just a fleeting glance and a smile, and couldn't believe how much he was attracted to someone he'd only seen for an instant years before.

It's her. At least I it is. He just couldn't be sure, seeing her sitting with the Knowles and their relatives. But he couldn't help being drawn to her lovely face. He decided that as soon as he had the chance he'd approach her.

"Do I ask her for a date?" he muttered. "Just how involved is she with that guy? I'll say something tomorrow. I can't keep putting it off," he declared, suddenly more hopeful about his future than he had been since he lost Chanel.

The woman and the man she was with were standing by the soda machine, holding hands. She'd been with him throughout the trial, so they were obviously involved. His heart sank. He'd hoped he was just escorting her to the trial, and they were only friends.

He knew by where they had been seated with the Knowles family that he was a relative or friend. That being the case, it only added to the reservations he had about approaching the couple. Nonetheless, both nodded in a friendly way, seeming to acknowledge him as Matthew Cook's attorney. He smiled back, trying to think of something to say as he went to the soda machine where they were standing.

As he was reaching in his pocket for money, he stopped and turned to her. He was greatly surprised to see she was staring at him.

"I hope this thing doesn't take my last dollar," he said with a smile.

Both of them laughed and nodded.

"Robert Wainsborough," the man said, holding out his hand. Kevin shook it. "The machine seems to be okay today, but yesterday it took me twice."

"It's got a mind of its own," the woman added.

Kevin swallowed. "For some reason I think we might have been in a Mr. Softees in Ocean City, New Jersey at the same time many years ago."

"Would that be some fifteen years ago?" she asked. She flushed as though sorry she hadn't pretended to search her memory. "Marcia Ramsey," she said, offering her hand. "Yes, I think I remember you, too."

Wainsborough cleared his throat. "Wow! That's incredible."

Although the man smiled, Kevin could tell he was wondering how they remembered a distant, one-time incident. Marcia's recall was much too swift and obviously caused him to wonder if more was attached to that time long ago. To be honest, it made Kevin wonder as well.

That night Kevin dreamed about a life that was no more...

Travel and adventure had nothing on Chanel's Aunt Eleanor and Uncle Frederick, her mother's older brother and his wife. The childless couple explored life to a fault. Uncle Frederick was a successful politician and attorney. Aunt Eleanor was an educator, and also wrapped up in politics, as well as social and civic matters.

The attractive couple took advantage of what life had blessed them with and traveled to places near and far.

Uncle Frederick and Aunt Eleanor had retired to rural North Carolina to raise ostriches commercially—the meat was gaining public appeal. Shortly after they were married, Kevin and Marcia drove up to visit them.

Three enormous dogs protected the property. "I thought they wanted to eat us," Marcia laughingly told Uncle Frederick and Aunt Eleanor when they came out and called off the dogs. "We came up to see your new ostrich operation."

As soon as the young couple stepped inside the ostrich pen, the huge, fierce birds ran at them, telling them that they needed to be gone, and fast. Thank goodness Uncle Frederick came to their rescue. He apologized and offered to lend them his motorcycle.

"You two young people came all of the way to visit, and there ain't much to do on the ranch," he said. "So you might as well take my Hog and ramble around these highways and byways." He smiled at their enthusiastic response. "Anyways, I gotta make up for my birds' angry reception."

After that rather scary experience the motorcycle had special appeal.

"Hey! Hey! Hey! Slow it down!" Marcia laughingly shouted behind him. Fear and excitement intermingled in her muffled voice as they rode against a high wind on Uncle Frederick's Harley Davidson.

He heard her soft laughter trailing on a breeze as they stopped for a picnic that warm, sunny day. His eyes were glued to her long hair beneath the helmet and her astounding beauty. Kevin couldn't believe how special she was. How lucky he was.

They were happy and free as birds riding that "hog" over the back roads and highways. During the five-day visit, Aunt Eleanor and Uncle Frederick epitomized the world's greatest hosts, treating the young couple like VIPs with meals fit for a king and queen. However, Kevin preferred to turn down dinner the day that Aunt Eleanor brought roast ostrich to the table...

Kevin awoke in a cold sweat, feeling immense guilty as he realized that, in the marvelous dream he'd just had, Marcia Ramsey had replaced his beloved Chanel.

CHAPTER 9

January 2001:

On the witness stand, Detective John Bowers nodded at the District Attorney's question. "Yes, I believe the person who killed Charlotte Knowles knew her." John shifted in his seat. "The decedent had on a Life Alert device, but she didn't use it. I believe she would have, had she come in contact with a stranger. Also, the decedent's cat took off for parts unknown as soon as the housekeeper opened the door for me and my partner. We were strangers to the cat. The housekeeper and the killer were not. According to the housekeeper, the tabby was beside the victim's body on the kitchen floor when she arrived the next morning. And from the blood spatter on his fur, it is apparent that he was in the room when the decedent was shot. There was fur in her hand from petting the cat, so the animal was with Mrs. Knowles when the killer entered the kitchen. So he was familiar with the person who came in and murdered his mistress."

John pointed to a table in front of the witness stand that had a cardboard box on it. "In that box over there is the loot that was taken from the decedent's home the night she was shot."

"Bailiff, please display what's in that box for the court," the judge requested.

A short, chubby, pallid man around fifty opened the cardboard box and lifted out the objects. First was a wallet. He held it up then laid it on the display table. The next things he took out of the box were precious jewelry, a Chinese vase, and some other valuables. Each item he took from the box, he held up and then placed it on the table until everything was on display.

"Detective Bowers, are these items the ones you said a fisherman recovered last spring and notified you about?"

"Yes sir, they are," John replied, nodding as he spoke. "If the person who killed Charlotte Knowles had been a drug crazed stranger, those items would never have been thrown away. I believe the afro-comb we found at the scene was planted there by the killer."

Lying in bed the morning after Matt's trial, Kevin still couldn't believe the judge had dismissed the case and told

Goodman that he didn't have enough evidence to support a murder charge against Matt.

"Maybe some of this luck will rub off on some of my other cases."

He had to admit, his two white law partners had done a lot for him, even though he knew they'd only taken him on so they could claim compliance with the ERA. Not that he would have had it better with any other law practice. But then, Robert and John had every reason to accept him, didn't they?

Ideally, he possessed everything they wanted in a token African American law partner. He was clean cut, with a medium-brown complexion, not dark, and close-cropped hair.

He also had impeccable scholastic credentials. And personality wise, if he had to say so himself, he was likable, calm, and reasonable.

Over his five years with the firm Robert and John had given him the kinds of opportunities any ambitious attorney would want. Nonetheless, all of his clients had been black.

But out of the cases he handled for them, one—where he'd defended a woman who'd killed her abusive husband—had affected him more than any other. It had come at a time when Kevin's wife, and the love of his life, was dying from Lupus. The abusive young husband had had a chance to be happy, to protect and enjoy his wife, something that Kevin could no longer do. But instead, he'd beaten her until she broke.

Chanel had been a sounding board for everything that took place in Kevin's life, especially his law career and his relationship with his partners, Robert and John. He shared his frustration with her at night and she helped him put things into perspective so he could make it through the next day.

One day, he'd overheard John saying to Robert, "Kevin gets this one for sure. There's no way in hell we're taking this one on. It's too racial and could be explosive."

That had been the case about the "baseball bat killing" in which a black boy beat a white man to death in a restaurant parking lot. Kevin understood what John and Robert were saying. He was well aware of the role he played with his partners.

When he talked to Chanel that evening about what he'd overheard, she helped him through the disgust he felt and told him that as an African American representing a black client, he was far better able to give the necessary support.

"Everyone gains in this way," she'd quietly explained and made it much easier to understand. She even showed him that while his partners didn't extend the professional life to a social one, and only involved him socially during the Christmas holidays, people had the right to choose who they wanted to spend their free time with, —or not—for any reason.

"It's just the way life is, especially between Caucasian and African American males. With both races, there is distrust and some form of dislike. It's sheltered, but it's there nonetheless," she'd said, patting him tenderly on his shoulder.

As he'd listened to his wife at those times, he was able to understand that as a black man he was a victim of circumstance. Hadn't he been racially profiled several times while driving in the city or on the highways? Hadn't the police approached him as a young man walking down the street?

And he could account for many things that happened to him as a black man that demonstrated systematic racism. So, as his wife so beautifully made him see society was embedded with the prejudice and racism ingrained in the minds of all Americans.

After that conversation with Chanel, he wasn't as suspicious and resentful when his partners handed him another case involving a sixty-five-year-old, mentally-ill black who had killed a white man.

Tim frowned in his beer and tried to concentrate on the ball game. He couldn't believe that punk had gotten off. He'd been so sure that Matthew Cook would be convicted of Aunt Charlotte's murder. A done deal—or so he'd thought.

Grimacing, Tim recalled how two days before the murder, he'd paid a visit to a barn that served as a hangout for a local white motorcycle gang that peddled drugs in the area. The mostly male group tagged itself "Bad Boys" and ranged in age from seventeen to forty. For years Tim had been frequenting the barn for his supply of methamphetamines and other drugs.

The motorcycle gang's hangout was on the outskirts of Briarton, near some dense woods. Ominous, dark shadows and chilling mystery saturated the area where the dilapidated, old barn stood. The thick woods suggested ancient ferns and seeping primordial waters—a setting for fairies, elves, and gnomes.

He'd tried to get the gang's help finding a 'hit,' someone to take care of his Aunt Charlotte. He never told them her name, just asked if they knew anyone who kill someone for a price.

"Dude, we don't get into that! *Bad Boys* we might be, but we're not killers."

Now Tim just hoped that no one remembered him asking about hit men. Now that Cook was no longer a suspect, Charlotte's family members would be people of interest to the police again.

February 2001:

John drove his 1995 Buick to The Barn, a local biker hangout. As he stepped inside the gloomy barn, the gang's leader approached him, rather cautiously.

"Howdy, officer. What can we do for ya?"

"It's detective. Detective John Bowers. And who might you be?"

"Butch. Butch Callahan."

"Well, Butch, I'm here investigating the Knowles murder."

"Oh, that rich, white lady. What they call the Valentine's Day Murder, right?"

"That's right."

"Well, what you want with us?"

John rubbed a hand over his chin and chose his words with care. "I figure you guys know your way around the drug community. Know who's dealing, who's buying." When Butch started to protest, John held up his hand. "Now, hold on. I'm not asking you to snitch on your friends."

"Then what *are* you asking?"

"We figure the guy who killed Ms. Knowles knew her, which means he's probably not used to killing people, being in the upper class and all. So I got to thinking that if he wanted to buy a shot of courage before doing the old lady, he might have come to you."

"You mean if he wanted to be high when he shot her?"

"That's right. But if he runs in her circles and knew her well, he might be someone that didn't freque—" John paused a moment, reminding himself to lay off the big words. These were bikers he was talking to after all. "I mean he might be someone who doesn't come here often. So how about it? You see anyone new around here trying to score coke just about that time?"

"No. Don't recall no one like that." Butch turned to his gang. "Hey, guys. This police dude wants to know if we saw anyone new around here trying to score a hit just before that old white lady was shot."

"He weren't new to drugs," came a voice from the back. "But he was trying to get *me* to do that hit."

"*What?*" Butch exclaimed. "Come on up here, Joey, and say that again."

A lean, hard-faced guy in his forties got up from his bar stool and headed over. "You remember, Butch. Said his name was Parker. I told him where to go to get some coke. Course, I knew Parker wasn't his real name. He wasn't one of us. He wasn't wearin' no suit or nothin'. But his teeth were too straight, and he just didn't look like us bikers. This guy wanted the best cocaine around. He said he was tired of meth and prescription pills. So I sent 'im to Cook. Cook's a cool dude."

"So you sent this Parker to buy coke from the defendant, Matthew Cook? This was before the murder?"

Joey scratched his ear and looked at Butch. Butch nodded and Joey continued. "Well, yeah, about a week or so, I guess. And while I'm telling 'im about Cook, this dude Parker asked me to do a hit on a socialite. But I told 'im, we don't do stuff like that. Few days later, I seen the police had linked my buddy Cook to the murder of a that white woman."

"Any idea what his real name is?"

"Nah, but I seen him around town, driving a fancy car, so he's got some money. He's pro'bly someone no one would suspect of takin' drugs. One of them pillar of the community type a guys."

CHAPTER 10

In the almost forty years since John had joined the Briarton Police Force as a snotty-nose kid of just twenty, no case had seized his imagination, or consumed him to the degree that the Charlotte Knowles murder did. Every day he woke up feeling excited about getting to work on investigating a case that had the attention of the entire country. And now that the case against the drug dealer had been dismissed, he had to start the investigation over again. Not that he minded. He lived for solving these kinds of puzzles.

When he'd first questioned Gwendolyn Knowles, she'd told him that her mother-in-law had begun to feel unsafe in her home. She said she wished she'd taken her concerns more seriously. But something she'd said about security caused a red flag to go up and he began to wonder.

He went back to the socialite's home. Lizzie the housekeeper let him in. During the investigation right after the murder, John had noticed the decedent wore one of those Life Alert buttons. He wanted to know why she hadn't pressed it if some stranger had approached her in the kitchen.

"Did your boss ever have to use the button for medical problems or any other reason?" he asked the housekeeper who still appeared shaken days after the murder. "You're sure the Life Alert was functional. It was working at the time of the murder?"

"Of course, I am. That morning, madam hit it by mistake and this man came on and said he was sending her help," Lizzie told him. "Madam was awful embarrassed about it."

John thanked Lizzie and headed back to the station. Once there, he checked the incident with Life Alert. They affirmed just what the housekeeper had reported. Just more proof the killer knew the victim. So who was Parker? One of the decedent's relatives, or a friend the relatives hired?

Either way, it was time to start putting pressure on the relatives. They had the most to gain. Picking up the case file, he headed for the interrogation room. "You're the victim's nephew?" he asked the man they had brought in for questioning.

Tim felt his legs weakening. He nodded a "yes" to the detective's question but kept his head bowed to avoid looking at Bowers.

If only I could stop my legs from shaking. Tim moved nervously in his seat. *I'd better get control of myself. I can't let them see me squirm.*

"Did you get along with your Aunt Charlotte?" Bowers asked next.

"Uh, yeah. I had no reason *not* to get along. Aunt Charlotte was a nice person. Everyone who knew her liked her." Tim wondered if he'd said the right thing. Sitting in the cold, metal chair, he cringed as a ball of confusion and fear lodged in his gut. He felt the way he had at the gravesite, as if his legs would give out any minute, and he'd collapse and fall into the hole in the ground.

He wondered how Gwen had responded when they interrogated her. She'd called and warned Tim the day before to watch everything he said, to be aware of every movement. "The cops won't miss a thing," she'd told him.

Tim muddled through the interrogation, but he couldn't tell if the cops believed him or not. Why in the hell had he let Gwen talk him into this in the first place?

"Hello, Mr. Knowles," John said, showing Justin Knowles the utmost courtesy. He was familiar with the Knowles, as was everyone in Briarton. And Justin deserved special respect as the patriarch of the highly-regarded family. "Have a seat, sir." He gestured and, once Justin was in the chair facing him, continued politely. "Can you tell me where you were on the night your sister-in-law, Charlotte Knowles was murdered?"

Looking at Knowles's pale face and shaking hands, John began to feel concerned for the old man's health. On top of that, he felt uncomfortable and reticent confronting a pillar of Briarton.

Nonetheless, he persisted with the interrogation.

Justin had had trouble breathing when he'd laid eyes on Detective Bowers. *It can't be him! It can't be, but it is. This is the guy I saw Sharon with that evening, coming out of the restaurant. Oh no! She threw me over for this...punk, this civil servant. Why? In God's name, why?*

He'd taken his seat, still trying to recover from the shock of seeing the detective and realizing this was the man his beloved Sharon, had chosen over him. The sight of them together had broken his heart.

He breathed deeply as his thoughts trailed back to all he'd done for her. Why, he'd given her expensive gifts along with cash, and had even sent her and six of her girlfriends on a cruise. He paid for all of them. His thinking was that it was better for her to go with them than with another man. She had pictures showing her with a slew of girls on the cruise ship, whooping it up. Anything she wanted, he'd provided.

And the reason that he'd been so generous was because he loved her, and he thought she'd begun to love him, only him. But she'd dumped him. After everything he'd done for her! Then one night, when he and Claire had dined at a wonderful, inviting restaurant alongside the Briarton River, he'd looked across the room, and there was his mistress with a man he didn't recognize.

Justin's stomach had lurched, and a sickening lump formed in his throat.

"Justin, what's the matter?" Claire had asked.

"Nothing. I'm okay."

"You don't look as if you're okay?"

"Um, it's nothing really. Probably something I ate didn't agree with me," he said, placing his hand on his stomach. "She's betrayed me," he muttered quietly to himself as the pain tore at him. *That cheap, dirty whore!*

He'd wanted to despise her, but he found himself, after months of mourning, missing her, lying awake nights thinking of her. He finally gave in and called her, pleading desperately, hoping she'd understand how badly he needed her. And to his great relief, she agreed to meet him. The meeting had taken place on the evening of February 14, 2000.

"Please, all I'm asking is that you'll see me from time to time, any time at all?" Justin's eyes filled with tears as he spoke, the word coming deep from his heart.

They were at an out-of-the-way, cozy restaurant in Bedford. They stayed until almost midnight when the restaurant closed for the evening. Nevertheless, at the end of the long conversation, as they were leaving, Justin was more despondent than before he came. Sharon had told him she had cleaned up her life for the man she loved, and she intended to be faithful to him.

"It's best if we don't see each other again,' she said. "I love John and he loves me. I'm not the same person I was before. I won't betray his trust."

No amount of pleading could change her mind.

The detective cleared his throat, jerking Justin back to the present.

What do I do? he asked himself now as he stared at Detective Bowers. *Do I involve Sharon and let her new love know about us? Or do I lie?*

John stared at Knowles, who still hadn't answered the question as to his whereabouts. He tried again. "Sir, we have to conduct these inquiries on everybody connected with the decedent. So, if you would tell me where you were, I'd appreciate it."

Sweating profusely even though it was a cold, wintry day, Knowles dropped his head, and then looked up at John with a sad, pleading expression. "I can't because I have a wife that if she knew I was seeing someone else, it could be the end of her. She's a very fragile woman, my Claire."

The man appeared to be under a great deal of stress, and John couldn't help but feel sorry for him. Plus, he thought, what could he gain by killing his sister-in-law? He wouldn't stand to inherit anything. Charlotte Knowles' son Brian got it all, or most of it anyway.

His better judgment told him a man of Justin Knowles' principles, a pillar of Briarton, just couldn't be connected to a murder.

"And you were with this other woman on the night of February 14, 2000?" he asked.

Knowles nodded.

"I see," John said. And he did. A man such as Knowles wouldn't want to sully a woman's reputation by dragging her into a murder investigation. That was the code of a gentleman, a man of honor. He studied Knowles a moment then sighed. "All right. Since I can't see that you would have anything to gain by killing your sister-in-law, I'm going to let you off the hook for now. However, if my investigation turns up anything suspicious about your relationship with the deceased, I'm afraid I'll have to insist on you giving me the woman's name. Understood?"

"Yes, thank you, Detective."

"Very well. You may go. Have a good day, sir."

Knowles couldn't seem to get out of that police building fast enough. He looked as if he were going to throw up!

Interesting, John thought. The man really should see a doctor.

Matthew Cook knocked on Kevin's office door. "The receptionist lady said I could come on back."

"Of course," Kevin replied. "What can I do for you, Matt?"

Matt took a seat in the visitor's chair. "I think I spotted someone I had some dealings with. At the trial I mean." He shifted nervously in his chair. "Remember you told me to let you know about anybody I associated with. That man had been ta my place more times than I can remember. I knew him as Brad Parker. But that don't have ta be his name. In my business people hide behind a fake name, 'specially big-time important people."

"Any idea what his real name is?"

"Yeah, I asked that bailiff guy at court the day the judge said I could go free. It was Timothy Knowles?"

"Tim Knowles? You're certain you sold drugs to him?"

Matt nodded. "Ain't no doubt in my mind."

CHAPTER 11

Y ou and I both know the person responsible for the murder of Charlotte Hornsby Knowles was not drug-crazed," Kevin told Bowers the next day. "But that doesn't mean drugs didn't play a part in the murder."

"What do you mean?" Bowers asked.

"Suppose the person who killed Ms. Knowles was not the person with the motive, but someone whose drug deals left him open to blackmail."

Bowers sat up straighter. "I'm listening. Go on."

"Check out Timothy Knowles. My client tells me he sold drugs to Tim on more than one occasion."

"Timothy Knowles?" Bowers studied Kevin with narrowed eyes. "Your client positively identified Knowles as one of his buyers."

"Yes. And the man didn't want his real name know. Told Matt his name was Brad Parker."

"Parker!" Bowers exclaimed. "One of the guys at The Barn mentioned a Parker. Said the man wanted to hire him for a hit on a white woman."

"Bring the witness in and do a photo lineup," Kevin suggested. "Include Tim's picture, and see if he can identify Brad Parker from the photo. If he can't, you haven't lost anything, and if he can, you've broken the case."

"Finally," Bowers agreed with grin. "So you think someone used Knowles's drug habit to blackmail him into killing his aunt. Any idea who the blackmailer is?"

Kevin shook his head. "No, but I'd look at the one with the most motive and the best alibi. Since blackmailer knew what was going down before it happened, they had to time to set up and ironclad alibi for the time of the murder." He headed for the door, then paused and turned back. "If your biker implicates Tim from the photo lineup, I'll bet the judge would give you a warrant for a phone tap on his phone. Then just hassle the man a bit and see who he calls."

Bowers laughed. "You're in the wrong line of work, councilor. You've should've been a cop."

Although he'd broken the case and had a good idea who had killed Charlotte Knowles, John took no pleasure in what he knew was coming as he drove up to Brian Knowles home. These people were pillars of the community—respected, trusted, descendants of the founding fathers.

Sighing heavily, he knocked on the front door.

"Come in," Brian said, ushering him into the living room and gesturing toward a chair. John lowered himself into the extravagant recliner.

Gwen and Tim were standing by the fireplace, Tim looking nervous and Gwen arrogant.

"You said you had news on the case," Brian reminded him. "Have you found the person who killed my mother?"

John took a deep breath. "We have. Timothy and Gwendolyn Knowles, from the evidence we have gathered, it is clear that you two are responsible for the murder of Charlotte Knowles. I'm here to take you into custody."

Brian gasped. "No! Gwen, you couldn't! You wouldn't..." When Gwen just glared at him, Brian broke into sobs and fell back into his seat.

"I want to know what evidence you claim to have that links me to my mother-in-laws murder, Detective," she said.

"That information will be handed over to your attorney, when you get one." John pulled out two sets of handcuffs. "Please turn around and put your hands behind your back."

"No! I didn't do it. You won't take me anywhere! You have the wrong person! He did it, I didn't do it!" Gwen screamed. She backed away, pointing at Tim. "He did it. Tim killed Charlotte!"

"You forced me to. You orchestrated the whole thing!"

Tim dropped his head in defeat as John began putting handcuffs on him. Then John read them their rights. "You have the right to an attorney. If you cannot afford an attorney, one will be provided by the state. You have the right to remain silent. If you waive that right, anything you say can and will be used against you a court of law."

March 2002:

With the trial behind him, and all had gone exactly as he'd hoped it would, Kevin was glad to be with his back home with his son. His mother-in-law had not missed anything the whole while she sat in for him. As a matter of fact, as far as Kevin could tell his son had received extraordinary care. Now though with everything settled, he was at a loss where Marcia Ramsey was concerned. With the trial over, everyone had returned home and things was back to normal.

How could he make contact? And should he make contact. He knew that she had an Advertising Business in Manhattan. She'd mentioned that in one of the conversations he'd had with her and her friend Robert Wainsborough during the trial.

Maybe I'll take a day trip to New York, give her a call, and ask to meet her for lunch or dinner? Having thought that, Kevin immediately decided that was what he would do. He could only hope that when he asked her about Robert, she would tell him that they were only friends.

Robert glanced over at Marcia and sighed. She was staring out the window at nothing, a dreamy look on her face. Probably thinking about that attorney. Again.

During the trial, he'd noticed that she and Kevin were attracted to each other. Once during a break he'd been delayed, talking with relatives, he came into the lobby to see Marcia and Kevin exchanging telephone numbers. Robert had said nothing, although he had an inkling that the interaction was more than it seemed. And things had only gotten worse. Her feelings toward Robert had turned cold. They had always enjoyed incredible sex. But, lately, instead of responding to his advances with passion and enthusiasm, she gave excuses or else just lay there while he did all the work. Apparently, he no longer satisfied her.

He loved her and had thought she felt the same. He'd planned on making her his wife. And then this. The pain was almost unbearable. He needed to end this charade and move on with his life.

He cleared his throat and shut off her TV. "Marcia, I think it's time for us to be honest with each other. You're hung up on that attorney. It's been clear to me since the trial. I kept hoping you'd shake him over time but that hasn't happened."

She looked at him then, tears filling her eyes. Her face was etched with regret, but she didn't deny it. After hugging her briefly, he sadly walked out of her apartment and her life.

Two weeks later.

Kevin felt he was living a dream come true that warm spring morning as he drove to Manhattan to see Marcia. The drive was scenic and had pumped his spirits even more, if that were possible to do.

On the telephone she'd sounded so glad to hear from him. *I almost didn't call her. Now, I can wait to see her.* He shook his head as he crossed the Tappenzee Bridge, thinking about what he would have missed.

It had been three weeks since the trial had ended and Marcia almost panted, she longed to see Kevin so much. Everything was back on track around Manhattan by now. It had been over a year since the 9/11 attacks that destroyed life for so many. She'd worked hard and her advertising business was not just up and running, it was doing better than before that terrible event.

Her life should have been normal. But it wasn't. She'd deeply regretted she had missed the chance to be with Kevin. She was persuaded he was the one for her, but she'd started to think she'd misjudged the situation.

That first time together she and Kevin dined at a chic restaurant in Manhattan. It seemed like they had known each other for years, and come to think of it, they had. Marcia couldn't wait to return to her apartment so they could take matters farther as they both wanted. They went to see a Broadway play the next evening. All in all, they spent a week together before Kevin returned home.

Marcia couldn't think of another time that seemed so deep, mystical, and magical. She couldn't believe how much Kevin had deepened every aspect of her life.

June 2002:

"I love it here," six-year-old Kevin Jr. blurted. His eyes couldn't take in enough. There was so much to see and do. He, his father, and Marcia had flown down to Disney World in Florida, and were staying at a hotel for the week. Once, when his mother was still alive, the family had gone there but he was too young, only two and a half, to remember very much about it.

Marcia said she couldn't stop smiling, she was so happy to be with him and his father. She'd said she fallen in love with him the first time his father introduced them.

Grownups were so silly, Kevin Jr. thought. But still, she was nice. Maybe his father would marry her, and he could have a mother again.

CHAPTER 12

May 2003:

Justin rose heavily from the leather recliner. He didn't know how long he'd been there and didn't care. He moved toward one of the tall windows, perplexed and deeply disturbed with all of the embarrassment and grief he had had to bear. The Knowles' fall from grace had been a brutal assault on him.

A heavy-duty pick-up truck rolled by outside. In a large wooden container, on the back of the truck was an animal trapped behind bars. The creature was a large, black bear.

Justin was amazed at seeing a bear being transported through his neighborhood.

"Why on earth is the driver bringing a circus bear here?" he asked in disbelief. As he leaned closer to the window so he could see better, the terrifying creature suddenly burst through the bars of its cage and rushed toward the house. The raging bear broke through the front door, snarling and baring his huge teeth.

"No! No! No!" Justin screamed, as he awoke from the same terrifying nightmare.

"I'm here, sweetheart," Claire said, as she rushed into his room at the psychiatric hospital.

The doctors had told him he'd suffered a nervous breakdown. That he'd become delusional, thinking a bear was coming for him. They just didn't understand the horrors that were out there in this life. Without Sharon, the world was a sad and ugly place. A cold place. But Justin knew he wasn't delusional. A bear was coming for him. It was called Death.

CHAPTER 13

June 2003:

Marcia took Kevin's hand and looked him in the eyes. "Kevin, I know that I could be a good mother to Kevin Jr."

She hesitated. "Of course, no one can take his mother's place, and no one should try to, but I'll love that little boy as hard as I can. And I know that he'll reciprocate it. We love each other already."

"Does this mean that you accept my proposal of marriage?"

"Yes," she said. She laughed as he wrapped her in his arms, happier than she'd ever been.

September, 2002:

The wedding of Kevin Johnson and Marcia Ramsey took place on a warm fall afternoon.

Kevin, Jr. squirmed in his rented tux. He was the ring bearer and had stolen the show, even outclassing the six bridesmaids and grooms in all their finery.

As the preacher droned on, Kevin thought about his life since he'd taken Matthew Cook's case and remembered how unhappy he'd been at that time. Now finally, his life was back on track.

"I now pronounce you man and wife," the preacher said. "You may kiss the bride."

As Kevin lifted Marcia's veil and pulled her close, Grandmother Ossie's voice erupted in his mind.

"Jes' a minute, we ain't finished! Yall haveta Jump the Broom. Come on, now!"

With a chuckle, Kevin whispered to his bride the order his beloved, deceased grandmother had just given him.

Laughing, Marcia requested the janitorial staff bring her a broom. And when it came, in what was an amazingly swift response, the couple did as they'd been told and jumped over the broom.

THE END

ABOUT THE AUTHOR

Loretta Moore is an African American female writer of many genres, residing in Dover, Delaware. She is married, the mother of three, and grandmother of eight. Moore is a multi-published author with several novels to her credit. Other published works include poetry, essays, and short stories in several magazines and journals. Wright also contributes to a church newsletter.

Moore is also a playwright and several of her dramas and musicals have been full productions. Presently, two of her plays are in the hands of theatres in Philadelphia, PA and Roanoke, VA. Ghostwriting is another area which Moore enjoys. She has a college degree in English and has received literary and theatrical recognition and awards. She belongs to an honor society and other laudable organizations, and volunteers in her community and church. Her interests include writing, reading, music, and attending theatre and concerts, as well as some involvement with outdoor activities. Currently, her next writing project keeps her very busy.